What Santa Forgot

Price Jett

DEDICATION

For children and their wishes. Everywhere.

(Especially these three: Rachel, PJ and Pete.)

.

CONTENTS

ACKNOWLEDGMENTS

For all their help, I owe a large debt of gratitude to a few, truly dear, friends.

First of all, to my wife, Deidre, who is my unwavering supporter, editor and friend.

Next, to the three little ones who listen so intently to all my stories and continuously inspire their old father.

Lastly, to Lorraine Tennison and Gordon Silver who were kind and gracious enough to edit the story line and make recommendations.

~

ARTWORK

Illustrations found in this book are by:
Michael J. Atencio. Washington, D.C.
Michael.J.Atencio@gmail.com

CHAPTER 1 -- JOHNNY MOSS

This is a story about three children who once lived on a street not all that different from yours. They had the kind of faces you might see any day on any given school bus. They had parents like those you'd see in and about your town.

They looked in most respects quite ordinary, but one night, they lived an adventure not one of them has forgotten, even to this day.

And since that night, if you looked carefully, you'd see there was something a little different about these children. Some said it was in their eyes, and you might see it too, if you knew what to look for. When they smiled, you would catch a glimpse of "something"—just there. And if you were there when they laughed, you would *have* to join in, even if you thought what was said wasn't all that funny. And right there, in the middle of can't-catch-your-breath laughter, you would see it undeniably – the twinkle that came to be.

If you ever find yourself lucky enough to have a "twinkler" for a friend, whatever you do, don't let them get away. They are the best kinds of friends to have, because they are givers. They give laughter and joy, and make memories so sweet you get teary-eyed just thinking of them.

But it wasn't always that way for these three, Sarah, Peter, and Little Dan. In fact, when this story began, they were indeed most miserable. And it was all because of Johnny Moss.

Johnny doesn't really come into play much in this story except for the fact that on this day, he made Sarah cry. You see, he told her there was no such thing as Santa Claus.

"In fact," he went on "there is no such thing as Christmas at all. It's just a made-up day."

Why a boy would say something like this to a little girl who was not even his sister is beyond me.

Now everyone knows that Christmas is the realest thing there is, in all the world. But as for Johnny Moss, I suppose he had never seen Santa Claus, so he just assumed there was wasn't one, and (I guess) went on to assume that the whole of Christmas was just another made-up day. (At least that is what I say to myself about Johnny Moss. Although I prefer not to think too long or too hard about people like him).

But the fact that he would go to such the trouble to spread his gloomy, terribly wrong-headed ideas to Sarah simply because he was unsure about it himself—well, that's the part that's almost unforgiveable. Because what he did, was take something special away from Sarah: her joy. And that's the really, really bad part.

As it often does, the bad news quickly took on a life of its own and began to spread like a shadow. Sarah told her brother Peter, and Peter told their brother Little Dan (which is what he called himself, being four and rather on the short-legged side). That afternoon found them, all three, sitting under the old apple tree in their yard, completely red-eyed and hopeless.

"Do you suppose you heard Johnny wrong?" asked Peter.

"No," said Sarah. "He was very clear. And when he saw I was going to cry, he started laughing. He said Christmas was something our parents made up, and if we asked them they would just deny it because they made it up in the first place. And then he said that I had better get used to it and stop being such a baby, because only babies believe in Santa Claus and Christmas." And with that, she burst out crying again.

Peter looked at the ground. Little Dan wasn't sure what all the crying was about. Being only four, he didn't have many Christmases to recall. He crawled over Peter to hug his sister, and said "Don't cwy, Sawa, don't cwy." (Little Dan had trouble with his R's sometimes.) "Cwistmas will come. I know it will! And Santa Craws too."

"Oh, Dan! Oh, Dan!" Sarah cried as she hugged him. Her tears dripped on the top of his little blonde head. "I wish this day had never come. I wish I had never heard of Christmas!"

Those were the exact words she said that warm November day, sitting under that old apple tree.

And just about then, a cold wind blew, rustling the few leaves remaining on the tree. November can be like that—warm and sunny until, seemingly out of nowhere, a cold wind stirs up clouds, and everything changes. Even the tree seemed to shudder, and not necessarily because of the wind.

November grew bigger and colder and suddenly, it was Thanksgiving.

Across the turkey, the children's parents asked them what they wanted for Christmas. Sarah glanced at

Peter. It was almost as if their parents actually *did* believe that Christmas was not just another made-up day.

Sarah and Peter named a few things they wanted and watched their parents' reactions. Mom and Dad just shrugged and said things like, "Well, we'll have to see about that" and "you never know."

And that was the problem—the "never know"-ing. Sarah wanted so badly to tell them what Johnny Moss had said. Yet every time she thought about it, she remembered how he told her that they would deny it. So she choked back the questions that were right on the tip of her tongue and went on eating.

Now, if this has ever happened to you, you know it is a bad place to be. And when you are in spot like this, the best thing to do is just blurt out what you have to say, no matter how strangely it rolls around your mouth or how clumsily it falls off your lips. Even if you just have to spit it out in pieces on the floor and put it back together again. That's better than choking it all back, because that makes things gloomier and scarier than they need to be. Yet that's what most people do, and on that Thanksgiving Day, that's what Sarah did, too.

CHAPTER 2 -- THREE DAYS UNTIL CHRISTMAS

"Fwee days until Cwistmas!" exclaimed Little Dan. "Fwee days!"

"What? Oh, right," said Sarah. "Three days." She got up off the couch and began pacing the living room. Their mother was upstairs folding clothes and putting them away. Sarah knew she had a just few minutes before she returned.

"Peter, do you really suppose Mom and Dad and all the other parents…." She had to include "all the other parents," for she could not bear to hang the blame on her parents alone. "Do you suppose they did make it all up? No Santa Claus, no Christmas… nothing, you know, kind of special about it?"

"Huh?" Peter said.

"You know, *Christmas*—or should I say <u>no</u> Christmas. Like it's all a big trick."

"If you ask me," Peter said, "Johnny Moss is just a big, fat liar. He cheats at football on the playground, you know. Dad said never to trust anyone who cheats at football. He's probably up to no good everywhere else, too."

"Oh, Peter, do you really think so? Do you really think he was lying?" And as soon as she said it, something started to bubble up inside her. Something called hope. Hope that Johnny was all wrong. She was feeling more and more sure of it. In fact, if they weren't on winter break, she'd go right up to Johnny Moss at school and tell him what a horrible boy he was! Didn't he have anything better to do than going around saying terrible things to smaller children and making up such awful things about other people's parents? She'd tell him that what he really needed was a day in detention. Maybe two days. And that his punishment ought to be to clean all the chalkboards and never be given ice cream again so long as he lived. Then maybe he would know how it felt to have something so wonderful as the promise of Christmas taken away when he least expected it.

At least Sarah enjoyed imagining all the things she would say to Johnny if she could. Then she felt a tad better.

"Unless…" Peter said. "Johnny *is* in the sixth grade. Maybe you know a lot more when you're in sixth grade than when you're in third. Maybe he was just trying to help."

Sarah fell right back into the dark gloom she had started to break out of.

Peter untangled his army men from a small net he had cast over them as a trap, rolled over on his back, and stared up at the ceiling. "Unless…unless we could prove Johnny Moss wrong!"

"Prove him wrong? How do you mean?"

"What if we set a trap?"

Sarah frowned. "A trap?"

"Yes! And what if in that trap we caught the very person who could settle this whole thing?"

"Johnny Moss?" Sarah began to imagine all the things she would do to Johnny to make him confess.

"No, not Johnny Moss. Santa Claus!"

"Yeah! Yeah! Whee!" shouted Little Dan as he turned on the spot. "We gonna catch Santa Craws!"

CHAPTER 3 -- LITTLE DAN AND THE GAME CUPBOARD

They spent the next three days planning what kind of trap they would need for Santa. Peter favored a net—he had been inspired by the soldiers on his living room floor. Sarah was afraid a net would hurt Santa, or maybe make him so mad he'd leave them lumps of coal and never come back again.

"The last thing I want is to be on some naughty list for the rest of my life!" she said.

"Yeah, that would be the worst," Peter agreed.

"And then we'd wish we'd never set out to prove our point at all."

"How about ropes?" Peter offered.

"Ropes?"

"Yeah. They could kind of trip him, and when he falls, then we causally come downstairs and say,

'Why, Santa! Here, let us help you!' Then, as we help him up and dust him off, we'll say, 'Wasn't it a good thing we were here to help you? Here you go, sir. Here's your hat. Here's your bag of toys. And don't you worry about a thing. We're good at keeping secrets. Nobody will ever know about this. You just be on your way with your deer and all.' Then we'll give him the cookies we had set out for him, and some milk…"

"Oooh, maybe I'll make him hot chocolate!" said Sarah.

"Perfect! Even better! And then when he's all dusted off and warmed up with hot cocoa and filled with Mom's oatmeal cookies—"

"The chewy kind?"

"Yes, the chewy kind! Then he'll zoom up the chimney, and quick as a wink he'll be on his way. No harm, no foul. And we'll have the pictures to prove it!"

"Pictures?" Sarah asked.

"Yeah. See, Little Dan will be behind the sofa the whole time with the camera. And bingo, we're in!"

"I'll tell you what you're in. You're in crazy land, that's where you are."

"What do you mean?"

"You just told Santa how great you are at keeping secrets, here you are taking pictures! And I'm not sure, but I think lying to the Chief Toy Hander-Outer is a pretty good way to get on the naughty list for good."

"But I won't be taking the pictures, Dan will."

"No way, no way!" shouted Dan as he ran behind the sofa. "Not Little Dan! You in cwazy land!"

The family's dog, Champ, a yellow Lab, lifted his drowsy head at Daniel's loud protests and sauntered over behind the sofa, too.

"Okay, fine, no pictures," Peter grumbled. "How about a video?"

"Peter, stop it! This is serious! And anyway, tripping Santa and then hoping he's stupid enough to believe we happened to show up at just the right time to 'help' him—I'm pretty sure he'll see right through that. Plus, what if he hurts himself in the fall? This will never work. Come on think, think! How do you trap someone without them knowing they've been trapped?"

"Bales!" Dan shouted from behind the couch. He went over to the game cupboard and started rummaging around.

"Bales?" Sarah asked. "Like bales of hay? That's almost as bad a ropes and nets. Besides, Mom would kill us."

"No, bales, *bales*! Jingle bales!" Little Dan stood up triumphantly, holding a little ring of bells strung together. "Bales, bales, bales!" He shook them and marched in a circle, singing, "Jingle bales, jingle bales, jingle all the day!"

Champ woofed.

"That's it, that's it!" Sarah exclaimed.

"What's it?" said Peter.

"Dan! He's got it!"

"He doesn't even know how the song goes! It's jingle all the *way*, not day."

"Peter, don't you see? What do they put on cat collars so you know where they are?"

"Bells?"

"And on cows?"

"Cow bells."

"Got it now?"

"So… you want to make a collar and put it on Santa?"

"Peter! Think about it. What if we put bells everywhere—on the tree, in the stockings, on the mantel, on the corner of the coffee table, all balanced just so—on the arm of the couch, maybe one or two on the floor where a black boot might bump them— over there on the edge of a present or two—under the tree—everywhere! And there's our trap right there, hidden out in the open. Anyone looking around would just see Christmas bells and happiness. Who would suspect that? Santa couldn't avoid the bells unless he walked through this room absolutely perfectly. Surely he'll bump one of the bells, and when he hears it, he'll take a step back and bingo! There goes another bell. Then he'll jump back and ring-a-ding, there's another! And before long it'll be jingle all the day— or night—or whatever!"

"And then we can peep out from behind the doorway and bam! There's the man himself!"

"And he won't know it was a trap at all," Sarah added.

"Yeah, he'll think he woke us up accidentally and he'll be all, 'Oh, I'm so sorry! Old Santa didn't mean to wake you up! I must be getting rusty in my old age!' He'll be so embarrassed and we'll offer to clean it all up so he doesn't get in trouble with Mom. Maybe he'll even give us some extra toys for all the inconvenience!"

"And for the rest of our lives we'll be known as the kids who helped him out that night he knocked everything over and made a mess," Sarah said. "And we'll be rolling in toys for the next fifty Christmases because he'll be so happy we helped him clean up quickly so he could be on his way.

"I still want to give him the hot chocolate and the cookies, though. It just wouldn't be Christmas without them!"

"Sounds good. Except I want to keep one of the cookies myself," said Peter. "You know, as a reward for helping Santa out after he made such a mess."

"Peter! What's wrong with you?" Then she picked up her little brother. "Dan, you're a genius!" she cried, and swung him around in a little circle.

"Jingle bales, jingle bales!" he sang, shaking the bells in the air.

"Hey, I'm the one who came up with the trap idea in the first place," said Peter.

Sarah rolled her eyes. "Right. Ropes and nets and you eating all his cookies—real smart."

"Hey! I only wanted one!"

And so, the three set about scouring the house for every bell they could find. They placed them here and there in the living room. Their mother kept moving them to safer places like the middle of the coffee table instead of balanced on the edge. She placed one safely up on the mantle instead of leaving it just so in front of the fireplace where an accidental jostle would send it rolling, tumbling and ringing.

"Oh, this is never going to work!" said Sarah after a while. "Mom keeps moving the bells as soon as we put them where they're supposed to be."

"And I think she's getting suspicious," said Peter. "I heard her whispering something about Christmas to Dad, and then I think she said your name, and I am 100% certain she said my name. And when they saw me listening, they went over to the other side of the kitchen and started whispering again."

"They're up to something, all right."

"Maybe they're figuring out our plan," said Peter.

"That's not good. Here's what we need to do: we've got to hide the bells someplace safe. Someplace they'll never suspect. Then on Christmas Eve, when they're asleep, we'll sneak down and set the trap!"

"But it must be before midnight," Peter added.

"Why midnight?"

"That's when Santa comes."

"Who said?" Sarah asked.

"Nobody *said*. Everybody knows that."

"Are you sure you're not thinking of vampires and werewolves?"

"Well…maybe."

"Honestly, Peter! There's a world of difference between Santa and vampires and werewolves!"

"Well, it still could be midnight for elves, too!" he protested, "They're kind of spooky, you know."

"Are we even from the same family? Honestly! Santa is not some spooky elf! Now, the one thing we do know is that he won't come until we're all asleep, or at least until he thinks we're asleep. So as long as were stirring, he won't come. We'll just have to stay awake until Mom and Dad go to sleep. Then we'll come down and set everything up, and we'll go back up to bed and pretend we're asleep. You know, fake-snore, turn this way and that, peek through our eyelashes, that kind of thing. Then, when the bells ring, we'll know Santa is in the house."

"Yes! And the good thing about this trap of mine is that even if we fall asleep accidentally, the bells will wake us up."

"That's the first sensible thing you've said," Sarah responded. "Except the trap was my idea."

"Was not."

"Was too!"

"Was not!"

And on they went, each claiming credit, as often happens when a truly brilliant idea surfaces.

Soon cooler sensibilities prevailed and they had to admit the idea had really come from all three of them. Dan's Christmas spirit deserved the majority of the credit, considering all his singing and jingle-bale-ing.

With that settled, they turned their attention to where to hide the bells so their parents would not disrupt the progress of such a brilliant plan.

"I do have that footlocker in my bedroom," Peter said. "Mom never goes in there. And we can throw my football uniform and flags over them." (Peter played flag football at that time in his life).

"Perfect," said Sarah. "Now let's find every bell we can!"

With renewed energy and optimism, they set about doing just that. Every time they found a bell, they imagined exactly where they'd place it, and with each imagining their hearts grew happier. They became more hopeful and so filled with the Christmas spirit that soon they were humming "Jingle Bells" and fa-la-la-something. Peter sang some twisted version of a carol about somebody smelling and Robin laying an egg. And if you were in that house you would have noticed that the whole place was filled with happiness. No one even thought of old Johnny What's-His-Name. (I told you he doesn't come into play   much   anymore   in   this   story).

CHAPTER 4 – THE NIGHT BEFORE CHRISTMAS

By Christmas Eve, the children had collected what looked to them like a hundred bells. It was really fewer, but no one actually counted. The bells were all safely hidden in the bottom of Peter's footlocker in a pillowcase, over which Peter had carefully laid his football uniform and his flags. If anyone had looked inside and observed how neatly the clothes were arranged, they would have immediately known something was wrong. Things were never neat inside Peter's foot locker. But no one looked in there that Christmas.

"Okay, children, almost time for bed," said Mom. For the first time ever they did not complain. They did not whine and ask to stay up late. They pleasantly and even happily said good night and started for their rooms.

"That's it?" said their father. "No fussing, no complaining? No begging to stay up a little longer?" He and Mom exchanged a glance and then looked at the children on the steps.

"Night, Mom, night, Dad. See you in the morning," said Sarah with a yawn.

"Yep, see you in the morning," said Peter. "I'm really tired. Really, really tired. Whew!"

"Night-night, Momma," said Little Dan. "We gonna see Santa Craws!"

"No, no," Sarah said nervously. "Santa is coming to see *us*, but we won't see *him*. We'll be asleep. Right, Dan?"

"We gonna jingle all the day," said Dan.

"But what about Santa's cookies? And the reindeer snacks?" Mom asked. "Don't you want to put those out?" For this family had a tradition of taking a small handful of oatmeal and sprinkling it around the chimney in the moonlight on Christmas Eve. As it lay there, pale and powdery on the ground, Mom would say, "There, now the deer will see this from the sky, and while Santa is putting out the toys, they can have a little snack too."

"Yeah, kids, don't you even want to do that?" Dad asked.

"Well, we are pretty tired," said Sarah. "And Santa won't come if we're awake, right?"

"Are these my children?" Dad asked. "You guys are usually bouncing off the walls on Christmas Eve. Where's your Christmas spirit?"

"Yay! Yay! We got Cwistmas spiwit. We gonna catch Santa Craws and put him in Peter's footlocker forever."

"What?" said Mom.

"Oh, Daniel, you are so funny," Sarah said, laughing a little too loudly. The whole brilliant plan was crumbling before her eyes. "Mom, let me put Daniel to bed tonight so you can, uh, get your rest." She couldn't risk leaving Daniel alone with Mom. He might spill everything.

"Well…okay. But not until we put out the snacks for Santa and his reindeer. Come on."

They all went into the living room and laid out three of Mom's famous oatmeal cookies on a plate next to the tree. Then Mom poured a glass of milk and placed it beside the plate.

"Okay, now for the reindeer," Dad said, and they all marched outside with a small baggie containing half a handful of oatmeal. On the ground in front of the chimney, they sprinkled the pale flakes on the frozen, green-black grass.

"See, these will reflect the moonlight so the deer can see it better from the sky," Mom said.

"Whatever gets him here faster and easier so we can get on with this," Peter muttered.

Dad and Mom exchanged puzzled looks. "Well, that's kind of the Christmas spirit," Dad said.

"We should go back inside, Dan's getting cold," Sarah said.

"It's not like he's going to get hypothermia," said Dad.

"What's hypothermia?" Peter asked.

"That's when you half freeze to death and can't feel your fingers and toes and even your brain goes numb."

"Ew, yuck!"

"Don't worry, Peter, you need a brain before it can go numb," Sarah said. She was now holding Dan on her hip and rather tightly too, trying her best to keep him separated from her parents lest he let other things slip.

Champ, who had followed them outside into the cold night air, sniffed the oats and then went straight back to the kitchen door and the warmth that lay on the other side.

"Well, gang," said Dad a little sadly, "I guess that's it. Up to bed with all of you. No playing around, no staying up late, no going in and out of each other's rooms."

"Don't worry about that, we're too tired" said Sarah, forcing another yawn.

"Yep," said Peter, "we're beat. Nothing sounds better to me than to lie down and take a nice, long, deep sleep. In fact, if we don't go back inside, I might fall asleep right here in the yard. How about you, Mom? Dad? Tired?"

Sarah cut him a glance that seemed to say, "And now *you're* going to give us away?"

"Let's go," she said, and with Daniel on her hip, she went back to the kitchen, Peter on her heels. They let Champ back inside. He was the only one in the family who actually was sleepy that night.

Mom whispered to Dad as the kids went by. Peter thought he heard something that sounded like, "Don't worry, dear, they're just growing up on us."

Upstairs, Sarah took the first watch. And this was their plan: they would take turns keeping watch on Mom and Dad until they had fallen asleep. Sarah would go first, then Peter, then Sarah again. Each was responsible for watching and stirring for an hour. The stirring was the most important part— they knew Santa would not come while they were stirring. They needed to arrange things so that everyone was asleep in the house except them. Then, with the house still and all its occupants dreaming of Christmas morning (not counting the wakeful children, of course), they would creep down and spring the trap.

Next, they would return to their rooms and pretend to be sleeping peacefully, as best they could. At this stage, they could let their defenses down, because even if they did drift off to sleep, as Peter said, the bells would wake them.

Sarah's watch was uneventful. She could hear Mom and Dad stirring and wondered if they ever would go to sleep. They didn't. Not on her watch.

She tiptoed to Peter's room. He had already drifted off. She rustled his blanket and he sat upright in his bed, legs crossed, and dutifully began his watch.

For a long hour, he listened and waited in the dark. Then he crept back across the hall to Sarah's room.

"Mom and Dad still awake?" she asked.

"Yep, and I could hear them stirring. First upstairs, then downstairs, then back up."

"Okay, Peter, you go back to sleep. I'll come and get you when they're finally down. Are you ready for this?"

"So ready. Tonight we meet Santa!"

Sarah checked on Little Dan, who was asleep in her bed. He'd been too excited to lie down alone in his own room just a couple of hours before. After pulling the covers up around his chin, she gave him a kiss on the forehead and went over to her door to listen for movement in the house. She lay down, resting on her elbows, her chin in her hands. After a few moments, her eyelids became heavy. She caught herself as her head bobbed. Shaking herself, she sat up, legs crossed. She felt uneasy, her ears too far from the door for her comfort. She lay down again, her head closer to the door, and put her ear right on the floor to better hear footsteps and movements.

Before long, Sarah was dozing.

She fell into a nice comfortable sleep, dreaming of a new bike and her history teacher, Miss Dryver, of whom she was quite fond. Soon everything was jumbled together in her mind, as often happens in dreams. History class and bikes and Miss Dryver were all woven together. She saw herself in a forest clearing, holding a stopwatch and shouting, "Go, Santa! Go, Miss Dryver!" In her dream, Santa and her history teacher raced around the edge of the clearing, almost touching the trees, which ringed it about. Santa was on Sarah's old blue bike, which was much too small for him; his knees came nearly up to his chin as he pedaled feverishly. Miss Dryver was on a new red bike, just the right size for her and with room enough for George Washington who was riding on the handlebars. "Go, Miss Dryver, go, Santa!" Sarah cheered as she timed them. "Go, Santa!"

And then she sat bolt upright. Santa! She'd fallen asleep! She jumped to her feet and opened the door. She could hear her father snoring. Finally! Her parents were asleep. She ran downstairs. "Oh, please, please don't have come yet!" Sarah whispered. She cleared the landing, ran into the living room, and switched on the light. To her relief, everything was as it had been when she'd gone up to bed. The stockings were empty, there were no new toys under the tree. Santa had not yet come.

"Whew!" she breathed. "That was a close one." Relieved and excited, she tiptoed back upstairs and went straight to Peter's room.

"Peter, Peter! Get up! It's time!" But he went on sleeping. She shook him by the arms. "Peter!"

There was no rousing him easily. She thought of how faithfully he had kept his watch, and how she had almost messed everything up by falling asleep. If anyone deserved a little more rest, it was him. So she crept over to the footlocker, reached under the uniform and flags, and found what she was looking for: the edge of the pillowcase filled with bells. She did not recall that they had gathered so many, but the bag was nearly full. Good old Peter, she thought, he's been adding bells even beyond what we found together. Arranging the bag ever so carefully over her shoulder, she moved silently toward the stairs.

The bells jingled a little, and that sound did more to rouse Peter than any of Sarah's shaking. He opened his eyes. "Is he here?"

"Not yet. You just lie here and listen. I'm going to set the trap. The next time you hear the bells, it *will* be Santa."

Peter smiled and closed his eyes, and with that Sarah was off. She began placing the bells in the living room. There were plenty of bells, so she lined them up all along the edge of the coffee table. Next she placed a few bells on the corners of presents under the tree. Then she set about placing bells on a few of the stronger tree branches. It was a tricky, wobbly-bobbly business that took her quite a while.

Sarah stood back and admired her work. "Oh," she said, "that tree is practically a trap all by itself." The gentlest of nudges by Santa would set a cascade of bells ringing so loudly, even the neighbors would wonder what was going on.

Next, she made her way over to the fireplace and the stockings, passing Champ, who was snoring. For half a second she was tempted to place a bell on his head just in case Santa stopped to pet him on his way out. But no, she thought, that would look too suspicious, a bell on the sleeping dog's head. The key to the whole thing was not to make it look like a trap. Now the coffee table just looked merrily decorated, the tree festive, and who would suspect bells on presents?

Next came the fireplace: should the bells go inside the stockings, or outside, but very near them? Sarah had been convinced that putting the bells in the stockings would muffle the sound, while Peter argued that if they were outside, there was no guarantee that Santa would jostle them.

As Sarah stood there thinking, the most brilliant of ideas presented itself: she could use the fireplace screen. The top edge of it was like a little black road with two bends in it. But the little "road" was very narrow, and balancing bells on it would prove nearly impossible.

"But the screen *is* the perfect spot," said Sarah. "They do say Santa comes down and goes up the chimney." She wondered how this worked, since their fireplace was gas and had glass in front. She pushed that concern aside for the moment; that was Santa's problem, not hers. As for the bells, if he did use the fireplace, he would have to pass that place twice. He would *have* to set those bells a-jingling. She took out one bell and did what she could never have done while her mother and father were around—she experimented. She placed the bell here and there, watched it tumble off the narrow edge of the screen every time, and caught it in the air before it hit the ground. But then she discovered that by placing it just so, such that the little crown at the top of the bell rested on the flat part of the fireplace screen, she could keep it from rolling. So she placed five bells just so, three across the front panel and one on each side.

She looked round the room at her handiwork: the bells marching around the coffee table, the presents, the tree, and, her masterpiece, the fireplace screen. She practically glowed with pride. This was turning out even better than they had planned.

She turned out the light and then lay down on the sofa. This was a change of plan, but she was afraid if she went back to bed, she might fall asleep again, and not even a cascade of bells would wake her, she was so tired. She'd miss the opportunity to see Santa for herself and offer him hot chocolate and strike up what could become a long and special friendship, the likes of which no child had ever experienced.

So she laid her head down on the sofa and closed her red, tired eyes.

She had barely dozen off when—

Ring-a-ding jingle, tumble, thump.

Bells were ringing and jingling, tumbling and jostling. Instinctively she turned to the fireplace. Those bells were falling even as she turned. But the sight which was the most welcome and shocking of all was the hole to the right of the fireplace. A hole right through the wall, an oval big enough to walk through. Through it, she could see the bushes outside, and the darkness of the night beyond.

From somewhere behind her, a red flash streaked towards the portal in the wall. Then she saw him. Santa Claus.

He was clearly rushed but his face was warm and friendly, and he had the kindest, twinkliest eyes you've ever seen. He seemed to smile and wink as he stood there in the portal, Sarah wanted to run towards him, but then, the hole closed up so quickly that it pinched off from his suit a shiny, ping-pong-ball-sized bell, which fell to the floor.

The hole was gone.

Then, it sounded as if someone was stuck in the bushes outside, or was at least having a sticky time getting out of them. Champ was so excited now that his front paws lifted off the ground as he barked.

Peter ran up behind her. "What's going on? Did he come?"

"Oh, Peter, did you see him? It was Santa, he was here—I mean he *is* here! He went through the wall, there!"

"I didn't see anything."

"Well, I did! Maybe he's still here! Quick, let's hurry outside—come on, come on!"

"Did you give him the hot chocolate?" Peter panted as they ran through the kitchen and out the front door. "Did he eat the cookies? Was he fat?"

"Come on, come on," was Sarah's only reply, and down the steps they ran. Looking up at the sky, they both saw him clearly now, as plainly and undeniably as you would see anything on a clear summer's day. Or perhaps I should say that Peter and Sarah saw *them*.

It was most certainly Santa, but also eight or nine tiny reindeer pulling his sleigh—slowly. They rose above the roof no faster than a helium balloon. They heard Santa shout as upward he drifted, "On Dancer, on Prancer, on Donner and…and …what's his name again?"

"Blitzen!" came a voice from somewhere in the back of the sleigh.

"Right, right—Blitzen!" And with that, as if the last word of some magic incantation had been uttered, the sled took off like a rocket. Only it wobbled and shook quite a bit, barely missing the power lines and scraping so hard across the tops of some trees that branches came crashing to the ground in a shower of leaves.

"Peter, did you see him, did you see him?"

"Not a very good driver, if you ask me," said Peter.

"Did you see his face, did you see his eyes, did you… did you see how they, I don't know, just sort of…twinkled, like he knew something?"

"Sounds to me like he didn't even know Blitzen's name."

"Oh, Peter! It was the most wonderful face in all the world—so kind, so gentle, so full of…something."

"Yeah, well, good thing he's got a helper in the back seat. I just hope he doesn't wreck that thing and kill somebody. Let's go see what he left us!" And he turned and ran back toward the house.

Sarah just stood there looking up into the sky, smiling, all full of warmth and longing.

"Come on, Sarah, it's Christmas Day!" Peter called from the doorway. "We've got toys to open!"

"Right, right," she said, watching him go back inside. But more than anything else she wanted to stay there and remember that moment. She had seen Santa, and he had seen her, and he had winked at her. He'd stopped and looked at her like he knew she wanted to see him—like she needed to see him.

When she went inside and into the living room, she found Dan standing in the middle of the room, looking up at the ceiling.

Sarah ran over to the wall and slid her hands over the spot where the hole had magically appeared and then closed so quickly on Santa.

"Here's where he came in and went out," she said. "That's why chimneys don't matter anymore. He's magic and can walk through walls, and oh, his face was so lovely and just so…beautiful! He went right though here and he looked at me and winked and then the hole closed up, only it cut off a bell from his coat and it fell right here. Peter, quick, let's find it! This is the proof he was here, I saw it myself!" She fell to her hands and knees, pushing aside the dozens of bells all over the floor.

"It should be easy to find, because it was bigger than all the others," she said. "It was shinier, like gold." But though she looked and looked, she couldn't find it anywhere.

"Peter, come help me! Oh, where is that bell, I know it was here—"

"Champy's got it," Little Dan piped up.

"Champy?" Sarah said. "Where is he?"

"Up there," replied Daniel, and he pointed at the ceiling.

And it was then that they saw what they still talk about today, even after all this time. Champ was floating, up near the ceiling, his legs now dangling, now paddling, his tail wagging. He circled and soared and dipped and glided with the bell in his teeth, casting a golden glow.

Champ was flying.

CHAPTER 5 -- OF BIKES, BELLS AND BLANKETS

"Look, Peter," said Little Dan, "Champ's a weindeer! Go Champy, go Champy!"

Sarah rubbed her eyes. At first she could not believe what she was seeing. But now there was no doubt about it—Champ *was* flying.

"That's impossible," said Peter. "Dogs don't fly."

"*Bird* dogs fly," said Dan. "And Champy's a bird dog."

"That's true," said Sarah, laughing. "Here, Champ, here, Champ! Come lie down." She patted his bed.

Champ rounded the ceiling fan and bumped it hard, sending the blades spinning. Then he began an unsteady nose-dive. One hundred pounds of yellow

Lab came barreling towards Sarah, swooped back up as she ducked, then rocketed down again, landing with a thump on the floor. He trotted triumphantly toward his bed and lay down with a distinct jingle.

"Wow, that was close," Sarah said.

"Yeah," said Peter, "he almost took you out. It's bad enough when he comes charging toward you on the ground, but flying through the air—it's like trying to dodge a Champy rocket."

"Champy's a wocket, Champy's a wocket!"

As the sound of his name, Champ stood and shook his head like he was a puppy again. Sarah tried to get the bell but he dodged her, jumping first left and then right, his tail wagging.

"Careful, careful! You know how he is when he gets wound up," Peter warned. "He likes playing can't-catch-me better than fetch!"

"Lie down, Champ! Drop it, drop it!" Sarah ordered, but he was having none of it. He was so excited, she expected him to launch into flight again at any moment.

"The last thing we need is him flying all over town with Santa's bell, playing can't-catch-me—"

"Yeah, or up to Mom and Dad's room—"

"Good grief, Peter, help me corral him!"

Peter, who loved Battleship and chess and all manner of strategy games, devised a plan. "What we've got to go is avoid making him think we *want* to play."

"How do we do that?"

"Easy, we just ignore him and soon he'll drop it. Then he'll pay no more attention to that bell than he is to all these bells on the floor. Follow me." They all went to the game cupboard and turned their backs to Champ. "Good. Now pretend like you're looking at games."

In a moment, Champ cocked his head, trotted back over to his bed, and lay down.

"Now's our chance, let's grab him!" Sarah said.

"Not yet. Wait until he drops it."

"That could take all night!"

"You'll see. Give it one more minute."

As Peter stood there waiting to hear the bell hit the floor, he began imagining what he could do if he could fly like Champ. Why, he'd be the most popular boy in school, maybe in the whole world! And in football he'd be able to block every field goal, intercept every long pass—he'd be the greatest player of all time! But then he remembered what his father had said about boys who cheat at sports, and he felt ashamed.

Behind them, Champ wagged his tail and raised his head. Then, with a sudden jingle-*pop*, a bone appeared before him. Not any old bone, either—this one was huge. Bigger than any bone you'd ever seen - outside of a museum, of course. It was about as long as a baseball bat and quite a bit thicker. Champ immediately dropped the bell and took the bone behind the sofa, where he lay down and began to gnaw as if there were nothing more important in all the world.

"Did you see that?" asked Peter.

"Champy's got a dinosaur bone!" said Dan.

"And I've got a flying bell," said Sarah, scooping it up off the floor. She ran across the room and leaped as high as she could, like a reindeer, and—thump, landed back on the floor.

She tried standing on the coffee table and jumped off, flapping her arms, and—thud, she landed back on the floor. She tried shaking the bell, ringing the bell, tossing the bell in the air and leaping up to catch it mid-flight, but all to no avail.

"Maybe you put it in your mouth, like Champy did," Dan said.

"I am *not* putting that thing in my mouth after Champ had it in his."

"I will, I will!" said Little Dan.

"Ew, yuck!"

Sarah tried holding the bell in one hand, then both hands. When all else had failed, she reluctantly held it between her teeth. Nothing worked.

"Let me try," said Peter. "Maybe it's sort of a puzzle."

"Maybe there's some magic word that makes it fly," Sarah suggested.

"Not likely. At least it's not necessary to have a magic word."

"How exactly do you know that, Mr. Logic?"

"Easy. Champ can't talk, but he was flying."

"Oh, right."

Peter sat down in front of the fireplace and turned the bell over and over in his hands. It did look different from the bells on the floor, and from all the bells he had ever seen. Though he could not say for certain, it sure looked like it was made of gold. It was big, about the size of a ping-pong ball, and there were four little slits on its sides. On the surface there were tiny indentations, as if the gold had once been pounded flat by tiny hammers. The gold was etched with carvings and beautifully symmetrical patterns. He tried to picture what the bell would look like if it were laid flat. He could even imagine how the tiny dimple, the crown, could be made by cutting two slits in the center, tapping it from the inside, and creating the little raised bridge through which someone could run a thread. That's how it would have been attached to Santa's suit.

Oh, little bell, he thought, *I wish you would reveal your secrets to me.*

And at the moment he thought the word "wish," the curtains of his mind drew back, and he seemed to know what to do.

I wish you would float, he thought. He focused his mind and heart on the bell, and it grew warm in his hand. Then it gave a tiny but beautiful ring, a sound somehow both ancient and quiet, and rose from his hand, casting a golden glow. It hovered about six inches in the air and then dropped back into his palm.

"I've got it!" Peter cried. "It's not a flying bell at all—it's a wishing bell, it does what you wish! Champ must have wished to fly around the room, and then wished for the bone. It's not what you do to it, it's what you *wish* through it!"

"How did you know that?" Sarah asked.

"I don't know, the idea just sort of popped into my head. That's how I made it float, I wished."

"That's perfect! Let me try!"

"I don't know…something tells me it's not quite that simple."

"Oh, come on, you got to try."

Peter shrugged. "Okay, just be careful and think it through."

Sarah took the bell and said, "I wish for a new bike," for that is indeed what she had been wanting all Christmas. With a pop, there it was in front of her— the perfect bike, as she had always imagined it. It was red, with a yellow banana seat her friends could ride on with her. It had a basket in front and her name was painted on the frame. You could never find a bike quite like this one in a store.

"Oh, wow!" the children murmured.

"Let me twy, let me twy!" said Little Dan.

Sarah handed him the bell and fingered the tassels on the bike to see if they were real. They were.

"Little Dan wants a goat cart!" he shouted.

Now, all Christmas season he had been saying this, and everyone thought he meant a *go*-kart—even Peter, who was always able to understand Dan better than anyone else. So Mom had bought a little radio-controlled go-kart with a blond boy at the wheel, who, if you used your imagination, looked rather like Little Dan.

But as a matter of fact, Daniel really did want a goat cart. He had seen one in an old black-and-white movie in which a little boy, not much bigger than himself, rode in a cart pulled by a goat. He'd loved how that boy had raced like the wind down a dirt road, dust and hooves all ablur, the boy's hair blowing and billowing around his head. And right then, as impractical as it would have seemed to anyone except a little boy, Little Dan's heart became set on having his very own goat cart. He had asked for it no fewer than ten times, and had even drawn a picture of it. No one could figure out his drawing. His parents thought it was a leaf until he objected, and finally Mom said, "Got it, got it—it's a very pretty go-kart. I see it now, don't you, dear?"

"The nicest one I've seen today," Dad agreed.

So they both were quite convinced they knew what Dan really wanted, and everyone went about their day happy as clams—except Dan.

But now, Dan and the bell were quite in harmony. With a pop, jingle, and a "baa," a goat and a cart appeared.

"Yay, yay!" Dan exclaimed with immeasurable joy. "It's my goat cart!"

"Mom's going to kill us," said Peter.

Little Dan flung himself toward the goat, brimming with excitement. The goat, however, was a little less enthused about popping into their living room and being rushed upon by an energetic four-year-old. Just as Dan reached it, his arms outstretched, the goat lowered its head and gave him a very robust, irritated, full-on head-butt. Dan flew backwards and landed flat upon the floor. He began to cry in protest and shock, as anyone would when the very thing he wished for turns out to be not quite as he wished it. It's even worse when your wish butts you back.

Then, to add insult to injury, the goat, completely unaffected by Dan's distress, sauntered over and grabbed Dan's blankie from his hand and began chewing heartily upon it, with obvious intention to eat it then and there.

"My blankie, my blankie!" Dan cried, and gathering his wits, he pulled hard on the opposite corner as he lay there on the floor. "I hate you, goat, I hate you!"

And with a jingle and a pop, the goat and cart disappeared as quickly as they had arrived. For that was exactly what Dan had wished for, holding his blanket in one hand and the golden bell in the other.

"Good grief, give me that bell!" Peter said. "Sarah, send the bike back too."

"But it's perfect!"

"Maybe it is and maybe it isn't. But it's not yours."

"It has my name on it!"

"All I know is we should send it back. I don't know why, I just know. Besides, didn't you say we needed to get this bell back to Santa? He's probably out there crashing into trees and airplanes and forgetting his reindeers' names."

"Oh, my gosh, you're right! We've got to send that bell back." She took the bell, closed her eyes, and said, "I wish the bike would go back the way it came."

The bell grew warm and jingled in her hand, and then the bike, the beautiful, perfect red bike with the tassels and the basket and the yellow banana seat, was gone.

CHAPTER 6 -- THE QUEST

"If we're going to return it to Santa, I suppose we should return it together," Peter said.

"Yes," Sarah agreed quickly. Both children were a tad afraid of meeting Santa—afraid and excited at the same time. "Or we could wish him here."

"Then who'd be driving the sleigh? It could fall out of the sky right through someone's roof."

"Oh, right. Then we go to him. Deal?"

"Deal," said Peter. "And I think we'd better all hold hands. Otherwise I think only the one who is holding the bell will go. But if we're touching, we'll all go together."

"How do you *know* that?"

"Beats me. Hunch."

They stood together, near the fireplace, near the hole that once had been. Dan was on Sarah's hip, holding his blankie tight. Sarah grabbed Peter's hand and said, "Bell, I wish you'd take us to Santa Claus!"

The next instant they were standing in a very dark place. There were streetlights in the distance. The children looked down and were glad they had their slippers on. The ground was not white, as they had expected, but black. As their eyes adjusted, they saw cars scattered here and there. They were in a parking lot. A very large, dark parking lot.

Out of the darkness, a figure emerged, dressed in a red suit trimmed in white and carrying a shopping bag full of presents.

"Santa!" shouted Sarah. "Santa, I knew we'd find you!"

"Well, you certainly did."

Sarah didn't know what she'd imagined Santa's voice would sound like, but this wasn't it. And he looked taller.

"You are Santa, aren't you?" asked Peter skeptically.

"Sure. But I really need to get going. It's been a long day, kid." He walked right past them and they realized how tall he really was.

"We've got your bell!" Sarah said, jingling it.

"Oh, yeah? Well, you can keep it. Merry Christmas. Now go home and go to sleep. See you, kids."

"'See you, kids'?" Sarah repeated. "That's it? We come all the way here to the North Pole to return your bell and all you can say is 'see you, kids'?"

Santa turned. "You've come where?"

"To the North Pole! To see you!"

"Yeah, all the way from Virginia," Peter added.

"Children, this is not the North Pole. This is New Jersey."

"New Jersey?" they said.

"Yeah, and it's awfully late. Aren't your parents missing you?"

"But I don't understand," said Sarah. "We have your bell and everything."

Peter quickly scanned Santa's suit. There were clearly no missing bells. "You're not Santa, are you?"

"Sure I am! Kind of."

"Kind of?"

"Well, I guess what I mean to say is, um—ho, ho, ho! What is it you want for Christmas, little ones? But make it quick, Mrs. Claus and our little elf are waiting for me back at home."

Sarah frowned. "Just one elf? I thought you had a whole team of elves."

"Oh, uh, yeah—right now me and the missus just got one. Emily is her name."

"Please, Mister, this is important," Sarah pleaded. "Are you really Santa? I mean the *real* Santa, the one from the North Pole?"

"Well, not exactly," he admitted. "I'm the Santa from Barney's department store over there." He pointed to the mall in the distance.

"But we wished for the real Santa Claus!" Sarah protested.

"Correction," said Peter. "All you said was Santa Claus."

"But why would the bell send us here if he's not the real Santa? It had to know what I meant!"

"Look, kids, I'm just on my way home from work," the man replied. "Like I said, it's been a long day."

"Okay, if you're not the Santa we need, then why'd the bell bring us to you?" Sarah asked. "If you're not the real Santa, what are you doing here so late at night instead of home with your family on Christmas Eve?"

"Times are tough in this town. This is the only work I could find. Sure, I'd rather have been home on Christmas Eve with my little girl. She's probably asleep by now. Sure, we didn't have Christmas Eve together. But we need the money bad, and sometimes, you have to put what *you* want behind and what your family needs in front. Know what I mean?

"Anyway, I'll be there in the morning when she wakes up and opens her presents." He nodded to the packages in the bag. "And by then we won't be thinking about the things we missed, only the things we have."

"But where's the real Christmas?" Sarah asked.

"The real Christmas was in Bethlehem—you know, 'O Little Town of Bethlehem,' 'Hark the Herald Angels Sing,' 'O Holy Night'—all that stuff."

"I don't mean that exactly. I mean the real Santa."

"Honey, the real Santa was some guy named Jolly Old Saint Nick, but he's dead. Been dead probably hundreds of years. There is no Santa."

"That's a lie!" said Sarah. "I saw him just an hour ago. Look, he left his bell behind! It's magic." The bell was warm in her hand and cast a faint glow between her fingers. But as she opened them, the bell went dark and cold.

"Just looks like an old bell to me," the man said. "Look, you children had better get home or back to your car or whatever." He glanced around the parking lot.

"Where *is* your car? Is this some kind of joke? One of those hidden-camera shows?" But the lot was nearly empty. There was only the flashing light of the mall security car patrolling a far corner of the lot.

"Look at you out here in your pajamas," he said. "You don't even have coats on. Where are your parents?"

"They're back home, sleeping. We flew here…sort of," Peter explained. He tugged on his sister's sleeve. "Come on, let's go."

"But that's how I know there's a Santa—because we flew here! Because of the bell! Besides," Sarah said, looking at the man, "I saw Santa, and you are definitely not him. You would never fit through the hole in our wall."

"A hole in—? Listen, kids, I've got to get home, and you should do the same. This is no place for you to be alone." He straightened up and waved across the parking lot to the patrolling car.

"Now we're really in for it!" Peter said. "Please, Sarah, let's go home! You've got the bell. Wish us home and we'll think this through."

"No! We wished for Santa so he must be here," Sarah insisted. "If it's not this guy, then he's just somewhere else."

"There's something wrong with that bell. It doesn't work right."

"It must be because it's only a part of Santa's magic, and he's out there with some of his magic missing! You saw how he hit those trees—that's because he left this behind." She shook the bell. "We've got to get it back to him, that's all there is to it."

"And all I'm saying is that we need to be careful what we wish for and how we wish for it."

"Oh, Peter, your brain is getting in the way. Listen to your heart—don't you feel it? Like we've got to keep going to find him?"

"Right now I'd rather listen to my brain, which is screaming, 'Let's go home and make a plan!'"

By now the security guard was out of his car and walking towards the children as "Santa" leaned against the fender, looking on.

"Hey, kids, you got parents?" the guard called.

"I'm not stopping," said Sarah. "I'm not giving up." And with Daniel still on her hip and the bell clutched in her fist, she grabbed Peter with her free hand and said, "Don't worry, Santa, here we come. Bell, I wish us to go to the North Pole!"

And with a sweep and a swirl, the children soared once and then twice around Santa and the guard, just like autumn leaves caught in a wind. Then they went straight up, and in a golden flash, they were gone.

"Did you see that, Harry?" said the guard. "Just like that, gone!"

~

The wind blew hard against the children as they
landed on cold white snow. Sarah held tight to Dan,
who clutched his blanket, which whipped in the wind.
The legs of Sarah's pajamas fluttered and flapped
violently in the biting gust. Peter was blown
backwards and went sliding across the ice. The

sudden cold took his breath away and his lungs ached. He could not shout. He could barely breathe.

Sarah turned her back to the howling gale and moved Dan to her front to shield him from the wind. As she renewed her grip on him, the bell slipped from her hand and went jingling and tumbling across the ice towards Peter. He snatched at it but it was no use. It skidded past him, inches from his fingers, and lodged in a large boot-sized crevice. Peter wondered whose boot could have made such an indentation in this patch of the North Pole's wasteland.

It started to snow.

Wind-driven ice particles cut across Peter's eyes so that he had to squint. It was dark all around but the bell cast a faint glow, enough that Peter could gain his bearings. The whiteness of the snow magnified its faint light, and he could see ten to twenty feet ahead. Sarah looked like a shadow standing in the distance.

Can't lose track of the bell, he thought, *can't lose track,* and he began to crawl on his hands and knees to where he'd seen the bell disappear.

Sarah was afraid to move for fear the wind would topple her as it had Peter and she would lose her grip on Daniel.

"I'm cold! I'm cold!" Dan wailed, his lips beginning to hurt and his little nose aching.

Peter's hands and knees stung as he crawled, feeling sometimes cold and other times hot. His legs were numb from the knees down, and his whole body ached as he struggled forward.

"Must get the bell," he kept saying. "Little Dan, Little Dan…freezing…" At last he found the spot, now filling with snow, and groped around the crevice with his numb fingers. They brushed against the bell and he heard it jingle. He closed his fingers around it with a handful of snow, and shouted at the top of his lungs, "Wish for someplace warm, Sarah! Wish for someplace warm!"

And getting to his feet with all the strength he had, Peter threw the bell as hard and straight as he could. Then a fierce gust knocked him back onto rock-hard snow. Peter could no longer feel his fingers or toes.

Magically, the bell landed within the folds of the blanket gathered between Little Dan and Sarah. Dan instinctively reached down and grabbed the golden bell. Instantly Sarah's feet lifted off the ground and they began to spin around.

The snow was falling more heavily now, and the wind was howling. It blew hard and Peter slid across the ice, unable to resist the force of the wind.

He could see them in the distance, Sarah and Dan. They were only a few yards away; he did not have strength enough to move closer or even to stand. He was so cold.

Without the bell, it was dark all around him. There was a faint glow in the distance, and he gazed straight up into the night sky. He was remarkably calm as he watched the snow fall and cling to his red-checked pajamas; to his cheeks and eyelashes. He raised his hand toward Sarah and Little Dan.

So far away, he said to himself. His thoughts were beginning to jumble, and for a brief second he imagined he was back in his warm bed.

But for Sarah and Dan, it was as if a warm, invisible bubble had enveloped them. They no longer felt the bitter air, and their eyes no longer stung. They could clearly see Peter and the brutal white landscape as they moved, inches above the ground. Sarah shouted his name. The blanket whipped in the wind and the icy white world was fast becoming a blur.

Despite their rapid movement, Sarah could tell that Peter wasn't moving. He wasn't flying, he wasn't glowing as Dan was; he was just lying there in the snow, his arm lifted as if frozen. He looked so small and so far away as she and Dan were whirling, flying, the wretched bell ringing. Then, in a flash, the barren North Pole was gone.

~

Sarah landed on a sandy shore with a thud and stumbled several steps forward. Dan was standing on a small mound, tufts of beach grass blowing around his ankles. He was looking up at her, smiling. Somehow he had gotten there ahead of her.

"Dan, where's the bell? Where's the bell? We've got to get back—we've got to go back for Peter! We can't leave him back there in the snow, give me the bell!"

"Oh, no you don't," came a voice from behind her.

"Peter!" She flung her arms about him in a fierce hug. "You made it! But how—you were—in the snow—"

"I think it was Dan. I could see you beginning to circle just above the ground and you were spinning further and further out, you and Dan, in some golden light. The circle got wider and wider and then you passed right above me, just before you rocketed straight up. And I saw Dan's blanket flying and flipping in the wind, and as it passed over, it brushed my hand, and the next thing I knew I was rocketing up with you, all wrapped in that golden glow. And then Dan and I were here on this wonderful warm beach, and after a bit, you came. What took you so long?"

"I don't know. But I was wishing and wishing to go back but I couldn't, and I kept grabbing through the air as we flew over land and water but I didn't have the bell anymore. And then as I fought the flight, it felt like I was slowing down, but Dan just kept going faster and faster, I couldn't hold him, and I slowed down and I thought I had lost you both and then all at once—here I was."

Peter grinned. "Guess I beat ya again."

Tears sprang to Sarah's eyes. "Oh, Peter, I'm so sorry! I should never have taken us to such a horrible place. I thought Santa'd be there and elves and a toy shop or something—something warm—and now all I want to do is lie down on this wonderful warm beach." And that is exactly what she did, burying her hands and her toes in the dry warmth of the sand.

"I did try to warn you to think this through. The North Pole is pretty cold."

"Cold? It was freezing!"

"Actually," said Peter, "I believe it is below freezing this time of year. Not good for folks in pajamas."

"Unless you're a polar bear."

They both began to laugh, imagining polar bears in pajamas. They were half crying, half giggling, as you do when you realize that some great calamity has passed—for indeed one had.

"Where are we, anyway?" Peter asked.

"Who knows? But it feels sooo good. I just want to lie here covered up to my neck in sand."

By now Peter was lying flat of his back as well, his hands thrust into the warm ground. He rolled over and looked at Dan, who stood on the dune throwing sand into the air towards a row of lights, tables, sidewalks and people about fifty yards from the beach. There was even a rather fat man with a white beard and a red stocking cap riding a bike along the sidewalk. He was wearing a brightly colored flowered shirt and checkered shorts, white socks, and sandals.

"Dan, when you caught the bell—when I shouted to wish for someplace warm—what did you wish for?" Peter asked.

"Flowida!"

And they laughed harder than they had in what seemed like a very long time.

"Thank goodness he didn't wish for a nice hot fireplace, or the desert!" said Sarah.

"Or a volcano! Boom! Boom! Boom!" shouted Daniel as he jumped up and down, shaking the golden bell hard.

"Good heavens!" shouted Sarah. "Keep that bell away from Little Dan!" Thinking of what they had just escaped, she added, "And me too."

"Throw me the bell, Dan," said Peter.

"My bale! My bale!" He jumped down from the dune and began to run.

Sarah and Peter, imagining Daniel flying to some place far away and all alone, began to chase him. With a splat, they tackled him to the wet sand. There was a jingle and a glow, and in a spinning whir, they were airborne again.

In front of a T-shirt shop nearby, decorated with blinking plastic garland and a purple Christmas tree, a pair of teenagers looked skyward as they heard Peter shouting "nooooo," but by then there was little to see besides a streak of golden light.

"Hey, cool, man. Shooting star!" said one of the teens.

"Yeah, either that or Santa Claus," said the other. And laughing, they readjusted their red stocking caps and went inside.

~

The children landed on a dark, grassy hill. There were no lights beyond the stars. There was a small fire a little ways away, the kind you make when you're toasting marshmallows for s'mores. Between them and the fire, a large stone protruded from the ground.

"Thank goodness we didn't end up in a volcano," said Peter, taking the bell from Daniel.

"Shhh," said Sarah, "somebody's talking."

They peeked around the edge of the boulder, which provided a great but altogether too close hiding place. Two men sat near the fire, talking. At first their voices sounded different, foreign, but within a few seconds, as a mist lifts off a lake, the language became clear.

"Did you see his face? It was…it was…just beautiful."

"Yes, it sort of glowed in this golden light…"

"And you haven't stopped singing since we left him, Simon," said the first man, who sounded older.

"Santa!" Sarah whispered. "They know where he is!"

"Indeed, I wish we could have stayed with him forever," Simon said.

"Yes, but we have the little ones to look after."

"It *is* hard to believe that one so…so small could be the one we have heard about for so long."

"I knew the tall one in the parking lot couldn't have been the real one!" said Sarah. "Too big."

"Do you think we will see him again?" Simon asked.

"I am sure of it," his companion answered.

"We are indeed lucky men."

"Yes. And I cannot wait to tell everyone that we saw him. *We* saw him!"

"Ooh, they are going to get in so much trouble," Sarah said. "At least *we* were planning to keep it all a secret."

"There will be time enough for that when the sun is up, Simon. We can go when the sun is up. The night is almost done."

"Almost done!" whispered Peter. "We've missed Christmas Eve in all our travels."

"Yes, but Santa is nearby," said Sarah. "They clearly just got back from seeing him. We can find out where he is and fly there."

"And exactly what are you children doing out here in the night?" demanded a voice behind them. "Here to steal something, I suppose."

"Huh? Wha—?" They turned around to see a man holding a long stick.

"No, sir, we were just—"

"Spying on us, that's what! And I caught you," said the man, tall and thin. "Come to steal what isn't yours."

"Ho, what goes on there?" asked one of the men from the other side of the boulder.

"It's thieves, Belshazzar!"

"Thieves?"

"Yes, thieves come to steal our flocks and our possessions!"

"Bring them here to me." It was the voice of the older man they'd heard earlier. "Bring them to me, Manasseh."

Manasseh, poked at the children with his stick and they all marched around the large stone. In the firelight, they could clearly see the two men who had been speaking. One looked about the age of their grandfather, with a weathered and kind face. This was Belshazzar. His companion, Simon, looked a tad younger.

Belshazzar smiled. "These are not thieves. They are but children. And look at this one." He pointed at Daniel with his staff. "He is so small he could not carry even a lamb away."

"We are not thieves," said Sarah.

"Manasseh, bring them closer to the light," Belshazzar said. They walked over toward the fire. "What strange clothing you have."

"Yes," said Simon, "they must be from a different tribe than we have ever seen. And a rich one, too, for I have never seen such colors and finery."

Sarah and Peter looked down at their pajamas. The men were dressed all in brown.

"What are your names, and from what people are you?" Belshazzar asked.

"I am Sarah, and this is Peter."

"And this is Daniel," Peter added. "We came by way of this bell." He held out his hand. The bell stirred and gave a little jingle, of its own accord. Then it glowed. First dimly, then brightly, then settling back to a gentle glow.

The men fell back, except Belshazzar.

"This is indeed a night of great happenings," he said.

"Are you from…from heaven?" stuttered Simon.

"Heaven? You mean because of this bell?" Peter asked. Simon nodded. "Oh, no, not heaven. We are from Virginia. Is this New Jersey? Or the North Pole? We've been looking for Santa Claus. This is his bell, and we heard you say you saw his face earlier tonight, and well, we just needed to see him too and get this back to him."

"Children," said Belshazzar, "I have seen no one called Santa Claus. The one we have seen this night is the child born in Bethlehem."

"The one who from of old was called Light and Love," Simon added.

Belshazzar continued. "Our parents and those before spoke of him, and longed to see him."

"They told us stories of him in our youth."

Belshazzar nodded. "Yes, and here tonight, after all these years, *we* have seen *him*. We were keeping watch over our flocks when suddenly an angel appeared, and a glorious light shone round about us, and we were so afraid.

"But the angel said to us, 'Fear not, for behold, I bring you tidings of great joy, which shall be to all people. For unto you is born this day in the city of David a savior, which is Christ the Lord. And this shall be a sign unto you: you shall find the babe wrapped in swaddling clothes and lying in a manger.'"

"And then," said Simon, "suddenly there was with this angel, hundred...thousands... saying 'Glory to God in the highest, and on earth peace and goodwill toward men.'"

"Before long they were gone," Belshazzar said. "So I said to Simon and Manasseh, 'Let us go to Bethlehem and see this thing which has come to pass, which God has made known unto us.' And we hurried as fast as we could and found Mary and Joseph, and the babe was lying in a manger. And immediately we knew, as we looked into his face, that something different had happened, in all the world. And we have told everyone we've seen between there and here—every traveler, every shepherd."

"Yes, and Simon even told the sheep," Manasseh put in.

"That he did," said Belshazzar, laughing. "And now we wait for the sun to come up and we will go into all the villages round about and tell them what we have seen."

Simon and Manasseh then each added their portions to the story. Simon told of Mary and how gracious and beautiful she was. Manasseh told of how he had spoken to Joseph; that he was a carpenter. How there was no room for them in the inn.

They each told of the angels they had seen; of hope for a new era in which God's love would be spread abroad to all people. They pondered over and over what the angel had meant when he said, "On earth peace and goodwill toward men."

The more the shepherds told the story, the more vivid the thought of the baby became in Sarah's mind. For an hour or more, they all laughed and smiled around the fire, hearing the story over and over. And whenever one of them missed a part, Little Dan would say, "Don't forget about what Joseph said!" Or, "The baby was in swaddling clothes, wight?"

The shepherds and the children talked on and on. The children marveled at how they had nearly lost this part of Christmas in all their talk of toys and gifts and bikes.

Suddenly, more than anything else, Sarah wanted to go and see the baby and Mary and Joseph. And the brighter this urge grew in her heart, the dimmer her desire grew for Christmas tree lights, lawn ornaments, and plastic deer. Even her anger at the bell and all their misadventures began to die away.

"The first Christmas is somewhere out there, not too far away, just over one of those hills," she said. "And we can walk there ourselves, just as the shepherds did. Oh, Peter, we must, we must!"

Listening to the shepherds and now Sarah, Peter's heart burned within him, and he too was filled with a sense of longing to see the baby.

"Children, it is a very long walk and you do not know these hills," said Belshazzar.

"Will you take us? Please, Belshazzar?" Sarah pleaded.

After thinking for a moment, he said, "I will. I *will* go with you, for I did not want to leave there tonight. Let us go now. The sun will be up soon, and we will have breakfast there in Bethlehem."

The thought of breakfast was wonderful to all the children. They were very hungry by now. Peter wondered what shepherds in Bethlehem ate for breakfast.

As they went, Sarah told Belshazzar of the bell which had started the whole adventure, and how after great cold and warm sands, Daniel had come to hold the bell. He must have recalled that the first person they'd met that night had spoken to them of Bethlehem and old Saint Nick. And then, Sarah said, Dan must have wished in his heart for Bethlehem, and that was how they had come here over land and water and years upon years and ages gone by.

"I should very much like to see this bell," said Belshazzar.

"Of course," said Peter, "but you must be very careful, for it has brought us many things that were like what we wanted, but not quite. It brought us a goat that tried to eat Daniel's blanket. It took us to a man like the one we were seeking but not exactly him; to a frozen North Pole, but not the one we were looking for. And even here, it has brought us close to Bethlehem, but not all the way to the baby. So all the magic was right and wrong at the same time. That's why this bell is so tricky."

"But if the bell hadn't brought us here, we would not have seen you, Belshazzar," said Sarah, readjusting Daniel on her hip. "And now we will see the babe in the manger—the real Christmas after all." She had almost forgotten about the quest for Santa Claus.

"Here, Sarah," said Peter as he reached in his pocket for the bell so she could give it to Belshazzar.

Sarah was contemplating the trickiness of the bell, wishing she had been more careful in her wishes. And if so, well, then perhaps she could have outsmarted it. And as she was lost in reliving all the regrets of the night – as Peter handed her the bell –their fingertips touched, and with a swish and a jingle the children were flying, or rather being pulled away.

Suddenly Belshazzar was left alone on the hillside, the Bethlehem moon just beginning to turn the corner.

~

When they landed on sand this time, they fell with a rather hard thump and a tumble. This sent them all rolling in different directions, bell and blanket and children alike.

When they stopped, they started to cry as if something very precious had been torn away from them. One of them was crying even before they'd landed. I will not tell you who.

The bell which they had each longed to hold at some point that night had tricked them yet again. Now they were farther away from home, from their parents, from their own warm, comfortable beds, and they had lost their chance to see the very realest of real Christmases, the first one.

Everything Belshazzar had told them echoed in their minds and ached in their hearts. He had told the story with such awe and love that they longed for their chance to be part of it as much as they had ever longed for anything they'd had and lost and wished for again in their lives.

And now, here, wet and cold, it was just too much, too much for three little, lost children to take in. And that is why they simply fell to the ground and lay there on the wet sand and cried brokenheartedly.

"What is wrong, my child?" came a voice from directly above them.

Sarah looked up in the dark. The voice sounded familiar. "Simon? Belshazzar? Are we still in Bethlehem, with Mary and Joseph and the baby, or are we lost again? Oh, Belshazzar, please help us."

"Children, I know of Mary and Joseph, and the babe as well. This is certain. But I am not familiar with this Belshazzar, nor can I recall ever seeing children in such straits. You look as if you have travelled many, many miles. You must find a warm place, get something to eat, and perhaps take a nap to regain your strength. Then we will get you home."

Home—home! The word sounded so good to Sarah, and she was so exhausted that she had no energy to resist.

"Come with me," the voice said. And an old man stooped down and picked up Daniel, who lay his head down upon the man's shoulder and went to sleep as easily as if he had been in his own bed. He was so tired.

After the man had taken a few steps, Peter whispered, "Sarah, let's get out of here."

"We can't, not as long as he's got Little Dan. And if we try to grab him back, we might end up taking the old man with us."

"No way! I don't trust him at all."

Sarah sighed. "I'm so tired, there's no fight left in me. He said he's taking us home. And I'm hungry."

The old man stopped and turned. He bent down, and said, "I'm hungry too."

Peter and Sarah looked at one another in amazement. They had been speaking so quietly, and what with the sound of the sea breaking on the shore beside them, how could he have heard them?

Ahead of them now was a seaside town, with houses lining narrow cobblestone streets. The old man strode down an alley, humming deep and low. The melody was unfamiliar but sweet, and Dan huddled closer, safe and warm beneath his blankie.

"Here we are," the man said, stopping at a door made of old, rough planks and crowned with a crooked lintel. "Effie, are you inside? Got breakfast on the table yet?"

The door swung open. "For you, it's breakfast, dinner, and supper," said a short, gray-haired lady with a round, pleasant face. "Any meal you want, and as much as you want."

"Well, my friend, how are you?"

"Can't complain," she said, "cannot complain one bit."

"So glad to hear it. Effie, these are my friends. Their names are Sarah, Peter, and Little Dan. As you can see, they are tired and hungry and have travelled very far. If you will feed and care for them, I shall return in a very little bit to take them back to their parents. And do excuse their very peculiar clothing. Their mother dresses them funny."

She smiled. "Anything for you," the little woman responded. Taking Daniel from the man's arms, she went back inside and laid him down on one of several cots lined along the walls. "Come children. Rest a while, and then I will make you breakfast fit for a king."

They stepped over the threshold. Peter, ever planning, ever careful, had already devised how, with the old man gone and the old woman not looking, he would take Dan in one hand and Sarah in the other and wish them all home to Virginia—taking care to call out the appropriate century and exact location and date, of course. He wasn't taking any more chances with the bell.

The old man was now standing by the door, the silhouette of his thin body against the waning night. "Effie, I thank you, and I am ever so grateful. I should be back before long." Then he thrust his head full in the door, the warm light of the fire flickering across his thin face. "Oh, and Peter," he said, watching him rummage through his pajama pockets, "if you are looking for this"—he opened his hand to reveal the glowing bell—"it's with me, safe in my pocket. You must have dropped it on the beach." And with that he turned and closed the door.

"But wait, wait!" protested Peter.

"Never you mind that," came the woman's hushed voice. "You need your sleep. The bell's in safe hands, you can rest sure of that. Now lie down and sleep a little while."

Soon, Sarah and Dan were fast asleep. Peter was too tired to run. Where could he go, after all? He could not leave his sister and brother, and he could not carry them. The only thing to do was to try to sleep and regain his strength, and then plan his next steps.

"Sleep, sleep," said the old lady. "Sleep is what you need, and then we'll have breakfast fit for a king. Fit for a king, we will."

~

Peter awoke from a fitful few hours of sleeping and waking, turning this way and that, plagued by restless, haunting brown dreams. He'd dreamed of a golden key that would get them home, but an old man stole the key when Peter wasn't looking and put it in his pocket. Peter kept grabbing for the key but could never quite reach it.

He sat bolt upright. The old woman was nowhere to be seen. Sarah and Daniel were *still* sleeping. Morning had broken, and light streamed through the windows and the cracks in the boards. He looked around the room. The fire had died down significantly, and the embers were piled in the hearth. A large stone table sat opposite the door.

His thoughts began to increase in number and direction. Flashes of New Jersey, Florida, and

Bethlehem, especially Bethlehem, ricocheted around and around. He reached into his pocket. No bell. He felt panicked again.

He heard steps outside and the sound of someone wiping and stamping their feet. The latch on the door moved. He lay back down quickly and pretended to be asleep, pulling the rough blanket back over his head. It smelled of smoke and herbs. He peeped through his eyelashes.

The old woman walked over to the hearth and poked at the embers with a long stick. Small, sputtering sparks shot up the chimney. She turned to the table and began shaping round, floury cakes.

"How did you come here—Peter, is it?"

Peter said nothing.

"I have never seen clothes such as you wear," the old woman went on. "You must have come from far away. By sea? Your shoes were soaking wet."

He pushed the blanket under his chin. The old woman had her back to him. He noticed their slippers were all leaning on sticks and drying near the hearth.

"My name is Effie," she said, her back still turned, her hands busy about the cakes. "Short for Eleftheria. Hope you don't mind I took your shoes off. I didn't

want you getting sick from sleeping in wet …. shoes
….. or whatever those things are."

Peter said nothing, hoping she would think him still
asleep, but steadily giving up hope that she was
fooled.

"Or perhaps you came by beast. But I doubt it, else
you would have brought them along."

Peter pushed the covers down and sat up. "How did
you know I was awake?"

Effie turned and smiled. Her face was round, gentle,
and kind. He felt completely safe as he looked at her,
more carefully now than he had last night.

"Well," she said, "this is the first time I've passed
your cot in the last three hours that you've been quiet.
All night moaning, mumbling, and rolling. As for
those two, in all my years I have never heard children
snore so." She winked, and there was a very warm
twinkle in her eye. "Just listen to them!"

They *were* snoring loudly. Peter smiled back. Just
then Dan gave a gurgling, rumbling snort and turned
over on his side.

Effie laughed. "Lands! Sounds like a little piglet's in
my cot!"

Peter looked at her full in the face and could not help but laugh with her, what with her face all flushed and her eyes twinkling so.

The room, warm and homey with its low ceiling and heavy, thick air, felt like an old, familiar quilt. You know the sort, with edges all tattered and worn, which smells like and reminds you of home. The perfect kind for curling up under on a cold day and pulling tight to your chin, or maybe clear over your head to make a warm little cave, safe and cut off from anything that could hurt you—well that was exactly how Effie's house felt.

Sarah and Dan were awake now, kicking back covers and stretching and yawning. They had had none of the restless dreams Peter had. They'd slept better that night than they had in a while. Perhaps it was because they were so exhausted when they lay down. They had dreams of shepherds and angels and faraway hills in the night.

"Hi, Sarah," Peter said as she blinked in the light.

"Where are we?" she asked. "Are we still in Bethlehem?" And then, seeing Effie and the room and the glowing hearth, it all came back to her—their landing on the wet beach, the old man carrying Dan through moonlit streets, the welcome cots on which to rest.

"Hello there, Sarah," said the old woman, "I'm Effie. Short for Eleftheria."

"Elef-what?"

"Eleftheria, but you can call me Effie. And no, you're not in Bethlehem. Is that where you're from?"

"No, we're from Virginia, but…it's a long story."

"I've got all the time in the world. How about breakfast?"

"Yay, yay, bweakfast!" Dan cried. "Do you have Cheewios?"

"What are Cheerios?"

"It's kind of a special Dan thing," said Sarah, not quite sure how she could explain them to Effie.

Effie busied herself with breakfast, and the children quickly warmed to her gentle face and eyes. She made them some flat cakes sweetened with honey, and gave them warm milk which did not taste like any they had ever drunk before (it was goat's milk). But they were hungry and Effie was kind beyond measure, stoking the fire and listening intently while Sarah told her the story of the bell. Sarah explained how it had taken them not only to strange places but backwards and forwards in time, and how they actually lived in the twenty-first century in a place called America. Just a few hours ago they'd been in first-century Bethlehem, not too far from the babe in a manger, and they'd been on their way there when, by some cruel accident, they'd been pulled away from the lovely hillsides and now found themselves here, with no idea of where "here" was.

And without having to say much at all, just by listening, it was as if Effie wound her way into their hearts, which is how some of the best of friendships begin.

Soon Sarah finished up her story and said, "Thank you very much for the warm milk. Do you have any more of those cakes?"

"We'd sure like to go home again, bell and Santa or not," Peter said. Only Dan did not say a word, as his cheeks were stuffed with the warm, yellow-brown cakes.

"My, my, children!" was all Effie could say at first. Finally, when the cakes were all gone, she said, "You have had quite a night, but it's morning now, and sometimes after a nice sleep and a getting-it-all-out, when the sun is up and the birds begin to stir, everything that seemed so black and hopeless at night somehow seems not so bleak after all."

And all the words she said, and didn't say, were meant to comfort them and make them feel that all would be well—for that is the kind of person Effie was.

"Besides, Old Nicholas will be back in a little while and he'll know just what to do. He always does."

Peter looked at Sarah. "Did you say Nicholas? Saint Nicholas, Saint Nick—Santa Claus?"

"I don't know about Santa Claus, but Nicholas, yes. As to saint, that I cannot say, but he sure is a very good man."

"So he's not Santa Claus. I knew it!" said Peter.

"I thought you were his friends, though. He knew all your names. Did you not know his?"

"Well, he sort of found us on the shore when we landed here last night at the edge of the water. You know, the bell…"

"Oh, I see. Well, you were surely fortunate you did not land in the middle of the sea, if what you tell me about that bell's magic is true. And you were doubly fortunate it was Nicholas who came along. He never could turn his back on children in trouble. And you seem to me to be children in trouble if ever there were."

"We'd be in less trouble if Nicholas hadn't stolen Santa's bell," Peter said.

"Stolen? Heavens, no! Nicholas said he'd be back, and back he will be. And he'll have your bell, too, or my name's not Eleftheria of Myra. I guess you really don't know him."

Effie stirred the embers, and the children watched them fly upward. She began to speak. "I've known him nearly all my life. We both grew up here near the sea, though at times our lives took very different paths.

"I always said he was born a child of hope. Many years ago his mother and father, bless them, wanted a child more than anything, but time passed and no child came. Then at last their hope and faith paid off, and little Nicholas was born, not all that far from here.

"His parents were wealthy, unlike mine, and Nicholas wanted for nothing. He was tender-hearted, even as a child, and he was ever looking out for others.

"Then, when he was in his teen years, a terrible thing happened. The plague swept through this village. Many people were lost. Nicholas's parents died. His uncle took him in and did as much for him as anyone ever could. But it wasn't the same as having his mother and father... you know?

"Anyway, Nicholas's parents had left behind a very fine sum of money, but the wealth never went to his head, as they say. More like it went to his heart. As he grew, so did his generosity toward others. Bless him, he helped people all over town, and never did he make an issue of it. Most of the time people never even knew it was him. He kept it quiet, you know, like a secret. Bread and meat here, wood for the fire there. And so the secret kindness went."

"And people never knew?" asked Peter. "He never got caught?"

"Just once—sort of. As the story goes, there was a very poor man with three daughters and a great amount of debt. Each daughter would need a dowry before she could get married, but the poor father would likely have to sell them off to settle his debts instead. And with no money, no hope, and no dowry...well, things were pretty bleak for the whole family."

"What's a dowry?" asked Sarah.

"It's sort of a sum of money a girl receives from her family when she is to be married. Without it, a girl has no hope of making a good marriage. And if she doesn't marry, she has little hope of any kind of a decent life at all."

"Well, that just seems too unfair and weird," protested Sarah.

"It's just the way things are here, little one. There are probably things where you come from that would seem 'weird,' as you say, to someone from the outside."

"Yeah, like football," said Sarah.

"What's football?"

"You'd never believe it if I told you. There's this ball filled with air. Grown men chase it from one end of a field to another for hours, and scores of people scream and shout at them."

"Hey, hey! Football is a tradition!" Peter said.

"Yep. Just like dowries, I guess," Sarah said. "Go on, Effie. What happened to the three daughters?"

"Nicholas heard about them, and he understood all too well what would become of them, and how cold and hard and hopeless their lives would become. He knew what that would do to those girls, how it would change them. How they would die on the inside, little by little. That's the worst way for a person to die, from the inside out.

"And so one night he slipped away with a pouch filled with enough gold (his own money, mind you) to make a handsome dowry and then some. He passed by the humble home and dropped the bag through the window. Some said he dropped it down the chimney, but it *was* the window. And it landed in a shoe which was sitting just there. Then he slipped away.

"The next morning the father found it and nearly cried for joy, as he knew one of his daughters was safe.

"The next night Nicholas did the same for the second daughter. But on the third night, the father sort of set up a trap."

Sarah and Peter looked at each other.

"He waited up and caught Nicholas dropping the third dowry through the window. By then Nicholas had given them more than enough to settle the debts and provide three dowries.

"So that's the kind of man he is: lavishly giving what some would dare not share partially, all to give others a better lot in life. Good old Nicholas! So you see, you need not worry about your bell. If he said he will bring it back, he will bring it back."

"Wow," said Sarah. "What makes him so kind and generous when others are…well, not?"

"I've asked myself that question many a time," said Effie. "In fact I even asked it of Nicholas himself. Best I can tell you, is it's like this. You said you were in Bethlehem earlier this night, and you wanted nothing more than to be with the babe in the manger.

You told how the spirit of that first Christmas sprung up within you as the shepherds spoke. Well, Nicholas has told me he feels much the same way. And while that first Christmas was more than three hundred years ago, we still tell the story of hope and love, and of seeking and finding, and of knowing that we can be better today than we have been in the past. That tomorrow can be better than today. This story has impacted Nicholas in a very special way. Christmas, it is said, does not come just once a year for him, but has sort of taken root inside him. And that is what makes Nicholas Nicholas, bless him.

"Anyway, the father and daughters never forgot what Nicholas did for them. How could they?"

"Yeah, how could they," said Peter. "So which daughter are you?"

Effie gazed at him for a moment, that endearing twinkle in her eye. "And how did you know that?"

"Simple. When you spoke of the gold being dropped through the window, you didn't say, 'Some say it was dropped though the chimney, some say the window.' You said it *was* the window. And when you spoke of the shoe into which it fell—well, you seemed so sure of it, as if you'd been there."

"You are a sharp one."

"You didn't say I was wrong, though."

"That's because you are right. I was my father's 'little flower petal,' the youngest of his three daughters. Nicholas gave me what I could not get for myself: a bright hope for tomorrow. And from that day to this we have been dear friends, as you might imagine."

"And your husband?" Sarah asked.

"He has been dead for many years now. And Nicholas stood by me through those dark days, too. He is a very good man."

At that, the door swung open. "Well, speak of the old bird himself," said Effie, and she shuffled over to the doorway to welcome her white-bearded old friend.

"Well, well!" Nicholas's strong voice resonated in the little house. "It seems a bit of sleep has done you all a world of good. I trust you found breakfast at Effie's house good enough?"

"Dee-licious," said Sarah.

"Better than Cheerios, Daniel?" Nicholas asked.

Daniel's eyes lit up. "Cheewios?"

"What are these Cheerios things?" Effie asked again.

"It's a special Dan thing," said Nicholas. "They're not here yet. But one day…."

"You see?" Peter said. "How do you know that? That Cheerios is a Dan thing?"

Nicholas cleared his throat. "Effie, if you will excuse us, we need to be off. Bring all your things, children—shoes, blanket, everything you brought with you and nothing more."

"But we don't have everything we brought with us," said Peter, thinking of the bell.

"Indeed you don't. You must be referring to this." And he took the bell out of a pocket in his long robe. "As promised, I brought it back."

"Where are we going?" Sarah asked.

"Back to the edge of the sea, my friends, back to where I found you. Or rather, where you found me. Do you have all your things?"

"Yes, we have them all," Peter answered.

They hugged Effie and thanked her for all her kindness. Then they began to walk back to the shore. Nicholas seemed to be focusing on something far out towards the horizon, though the children could see nothing there.

"Nicholas, I have a question for you," Peter said.

"I'm sure you do, Peter. We will have time enough for all your questions. I will answer those I can; for some, I will have to ask your pardon, perhaps. But for now, if you will indulge me just a few more minutes of quiet, I am trying to piece together our most important next steps."

By the time they reached the shore, Nicholas was his old cheerful self again. "Here we are," he said. "This is where we found each other last night, is it not?"

"Yes, this is where we sort of…landed," said Sarah. "Do you know where our house is and how to get there?"

"Some things we can never know with absolute certainty, but we can know enough. And that is where faith comes in, to carry us the last mile. As to your question, yes, I know enough to get you home, of that I am certain. Home is closer than you think, children. Now I believe the silent one here—who is deep in thought, if I am reading him correctly—had a few questions."

"Well, yes," said Peter. "Three, actually."

"Only three? Go on."

Peter cleared his throat. "One, why did you take the bell? And two, how did you know our names, and all about Cheerios and Little Dan, before we even told you?"

"Well, as to your first question, why do you think I took the bell?"

"At first I thought you wanted it because it was gold or because it glowed. But now, after hearing Effie, I don't think that's it."

"What do you think now?"

"I think maybe you were trying to prevent us from hurting ourselves by using it again."

"That is correct, partially. But I could also sense that the bell was not of this world, and I suspected it had something to do with your future and mine. I thought it was best to set it aside and consider it a little before getting too deeply involved."

"So that is what you were doing last night? Considering it?"

"Yes, that's a good way to put it. Considering it."

"And is that how you knew so much about us? Like Dan's Cheerios?" Peter asked.

"It certainly didn't hurt," Nicholas replied with a wink. "I am afraid I can go no further there. But that is only two questions. You said you had three."

"The third is this—are you Santa Claus? I mean, are you *the* Saint Nicholas?"

"I will answer your question with a question. Your brother here, is he called Mr. Dan or Little Dan?"

Peter frowned. "Well…he is Little Dan, for now. Maybe people will call him Mr. Dan when he's older."

"Then you have answered your own question. For now, I am just Nicholas."

"Then what about Santa Claus?"

"That is the inevitable question, is it not? I will explain it to you this way." Nicholas looked off into the distance. "There will be many Santa Clauses, Saint Nicholases, Sinter Klauses, and Father Christmases in the world. Call them helpers, if you like. You even met one earlier in the parking lot."

"You know about that, too?" Peter asked. Nicholas smiled. "But he wasn't the *real* one—I mean, he wasn't you, giving people meals and firewood and dowries and all that."

"I see you know a little about me as well."

"It was Effie," said Sarah. "She…"

Nicholas chuckled. "Good old Effie. You are right, the man in the parking lot was not me. But that's not to say he wasn't giving important things. Even to you."

"So these other Santa Clauses, they are like you but not exactly you? Maybe…pretending to be you?" Sarah asked.

"Yeah, the one in the parking lot had a fake beard," Peter said.

"But was not his heart genuine? Didn't he try to keep you safe by delaying you a while until the officer came?"

"Yeah, he did."

"And didn't he sacrifice his own Christmas Eve to provide for his family's needs?"

"I remember," said Sarah. "He said something like, 'Sometimes you have to put what you want behind you, and what your family needs in front.'"

"And that's just what Peter did for you in the North Pole," Nicholas said. "I dare say he saved your lives."

Peter stared at the ground, though he felt very warm inside. "I was afraid Little Dan was going to freeze to death ….. or something."

"Those *were* very Nicholas kinds of things to do," Sarah told Peter.

Nicholas winked. "Thank you, my dear. That is indeed a high compliment, comparing me to Peter."

"So all these Sinter Klauses and Saint Nicks, they point back to you in a way," Sarah said. "And all the gifts and boxes and bows…"

"Well, little one, here's how I think about it. There's a great river which flows across time. It's the story of man and all his greatness and all his terribleness at the same time. It's the story that we are not alone. That someone watches over us. And that someone sees all the good and all the bad, but especially looks for the good in us. And I and all the Santas who will come after me (and all the Christmas gifts and boxes and bows)—they are all pointers to the thing at the center of that eternal story of man – to that one best gift sent down from the Father of Lights…"

"Love?" Sarah interrupted.

"Yes, love, in a manner of speaking. Love and faith and a bright hope for tomorrow, all wrapped up so neatly in swaddling clothes so very long ago.

"Now I believe that is all the time we have for questions. Unless, of course, *you* have a question," he said, rubbing Little Dan on the top of his head.

"I have a question," said Dan, raising his hand as if he were in preschool. This made Nicholas laugh.

"You do? What is it?"

Dan gazed into Nicholas's face. "Did your Momma have bwown eyes? My momma's eyes are bwown."

"Ah, Little Dan, you have asked me a very hard question. I suppose they were. At least I think they were. I am an old man and I have thought of my mother and my father many times over the years. I have tried time without end to recall their faces and their voices. They were taken so unexpectedly from me when I was a boy that… well, I had no time to gather up all the memories I might have wanted one day. I cannot tell you how many times I have wished to bring some memory to life again, or to go and see them. But where they have gone, I cannot go. Not yet. And alas, with each passing year, the few pieces I can recall become fainter and dimmer. I can no longer even recall their voices. To hear my mother's voice again and to see her eyes—that would be worth all the gifts I have ever received."

"Me too," said Daniel. "I miss Momma."

"I understand, my boy. I understand. Let us see what we can do about that."

CHAPTER 7 -- BACKWARDS AND FORWARDS AND HOME AGAIN

Standing on the edge of the sea, Nicholas said: "Children, we have come far enough. You must now make one last wish. And that is to go forward, to go back home again. Further, you must wish that all you have already wished would be undone as if you had never wished it in the first place, for that is the only way to set things right. I fear that all your hopping backward and forward across time and places may have created ripples, the impact of which would be hard to know."

"Oh, Nicholas, will you make the wish for us?" Sarah asked. "We seem to land in awful situations every time we try to use the bell."

To their surprise, he said, "No, children, I cannot. You must own your own wishes and dreams. And you must also wish to leave the bell behind with me. I will get it to where it belongs, to its rightful owner. This must be the last time you use it."

"But these are many wishes, not just one," said Peter.

"And the minute we wish the first wish," said Sarah, "everything starts spinning and ringing and we get swept away into some other predicament that gets us farther away from our real wish. And farther away from home. Farther away from Mom and Dad. Please, can't you help us?"

Nicholas could practically never deny a child anything, and especially not these three. They wanted nothing more than to set things right and get back to their mom and dad. Their longing was something he understood deeply, for he could barely recall his own parents and his heart ached whenever he tried. He reached out and placed the bell in Peter's hand. Looking him squarely in the face, eyes twinkling, he said, "Peter, listen carefully to me. Think hard. The way home is inside you. Think about it the way only you can. Your brain is wired perfectly for a puzzle like this. The answer is not far from you."

"Me?" Peter was shocked that Nicholas was so sure he was the answer.

"I believe in you, Peter."

"And I believe in you too, Nicholas."

Peter shut his eyes. Nicholas' faith in him gave him faith in himself. In a moment, he opened his eyes and said, "I think I'm ready."

Peter put Daniel on his hip and took Sarah's right hand in his left. Then, gripping the bell tightly in his hand, he looked into Nicholas' face.

"Be careful, Peter," said Sarah.

"Go, Peter! Go, Peter!" Little Dan cheered.

Peter began to speak, and they all fell silent. "Listen to me, bell." He furrowed his brow, staring at the bell as if it were a chess player he dared not underestimate. "My wish is long and complicated. It is a bundle of wishes inside one wish. But first there are two conditions. One: only the wishes I make aloud are to be fulfilled, and not any other wish that may be in my heart. Got it?"

The bell did not move.

"The second condition is that this wish would only be completely fulfilled when I speak the word that is spelled in English d-o-n-e."

(Peter was afraid that if he said the word "done" out loud, the wish would be over before it had even begun. He wasn't sure if condition number two was really necessary, but given all they had been through, he wanted to take no chances.)

Nicholas smiled. Peter continued very slowly, his thoughts falling in line.

"Okay. The first wish inside my master wish is that we would return home to the time and place where this adventure of ours started—and by 'we' and 'ours' I mean Sarah and Little Dan and myself, and all the things we brought with us when the wishing began. Except for you, bell, but I will get to you in a moment."

The bell began to warm in his hand as if it could not wait to begin working its magic, but was restrained.

Peter continued nervously. "Second, I wish that all our wishes prior to this one would be unwound, and all unexpected parts of those wishes would also be unwound, as if the chalkboard of our wishes were erased clean." This part seemed to particularly delight Nicholas.

"Third, I wish that you, golden bell, would be left behind with Nicholas and not travel back with us." That was the hardest part, for a small part of him did want to bring the wishing bell back with them.

By now, the bell was growing warmer and hotter by the second, and it started to jingle ever so slightly.

Then Peter was ready to make the easiest wish of all—easy because as he spoke it aloud, he felt it in his heart at the same time.

He paused.

Nicholas looked at him, puzzled. To his mind, Peter had wrapped everything up neatly.

Peter spoke quickly now. "And last, I wish that this Christmas, Nicholas would clearly and completely recall all the sweetest memories of his mother and father, no matter how long ago those memories were lost."

And with that he shouted, "Done!"

In a swirl of spinning and ringing, the world began to sweep before the children's eyes. They could feel and see that they were moving again with great speed across lands and waters and dark skies. And the last thing they remembered, just before the bell's magic swept them away, were Nicholas's eyes. Peter was sure beyond sure that those eyes were wet as they smiled and twinkled back at him.

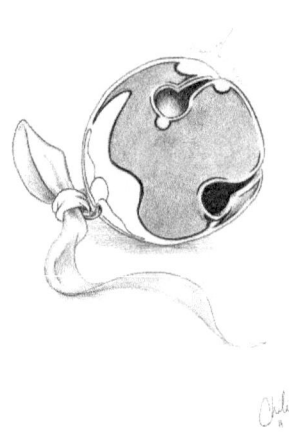

CHAPTER 8 – CHRISTMAS DAY

Sarah opened her eyes and found herself in her room. She was lying on the floor, stiff and cold, her ear pressed to the carpet.

"Peter! Peter!" she cried, jumping to her feet and running into the hall.

Dan was wide awake and mumbling grumpily, "Momma, Momma."

They ran downstairs quick as a wink to find Mom and Dad sitting in the kitchen in their pajamas. Dad was holding the video camera to catch their reactions as he always did, "to store up for their tomorrows, the swiftness of Christmas morning".

The children fled without speaking to the living room, and there were toys and ribbons and boxes and overfilled stockings hanging from the mantel. Sarah went to the wall to the right of the fireplace and smoothed her hand over the hole she had seen the night before—or rather thought she had seen. There were no bells on the fireplace screen.

"A dream," she said. "It was all a dream."

"What was a dream?" said Mom.

"Oh—nothing." With each passing second, Sarah felt all her memories of the previous night slipping away, as often happens when one wakes from a beautiful dream. You know how it is when there is a dream in your head so lovely that you want nothing more than to hold on to it, but the more you grab at it with the fingers of your mind, the more it crumbles like the ashes left behind when a piece of paper has burned. It curls up like a shadow of what it once was. And you know that if you ever touched it, no matter how gently, the whole thing would crumble. That's exactly how she felt.

Sarah turned around. "Peter, did you have a dream last night?"

"I did. But I can't remember all of it, just parts. How did you know?" he asked.

She shrugged her shoulders. "Hunch."

They spent the rest of morning opening presents and being filmed by Dad. But most of all, they felt lovely and loved. In fact, that's just the way they described it years later. "I felt so lovely and so loved," Sarah would often say of that Christmas.

But as the morning progressed, glimpses of twinkling eyes and snatches of conversations floated through the children's minds. And with every "I love you," with every gift, every box, ribbon, and bow—and especially with every bell—memories flickered. And the same dream they'd thought was crumbling began to reconstruct itself in their hearts and in their minds, one small piece at a time.

Soon all the opening was done and papers lay strewn across the floor as if a package-opening whirlwind (or three of them) had swept through the living room. Then Daniel headed over to the game cupboard behind the sofa. Something was there he had left behind and needed to find again.

"Whee, whee! Jingle bales, jingle bales, jingle all the day!" He came out from between the sofa and the cupboard, not walking now but draped over Champ's back, his ring of bells in his hand. "Whee, whee!" he shouted as he rolled to the floor.

Unencumbered by his passenger, Champ disappeared around the corner carrying just about the largest bone you have ever seen—outside of a museum, of course.

The End.

ABOUT THE AUTHOR

Price Jett lives in Virginia with his wife, Deidre, three children, two cows (Rosie and Cotton) and, once upon a time, a dog named Champ.